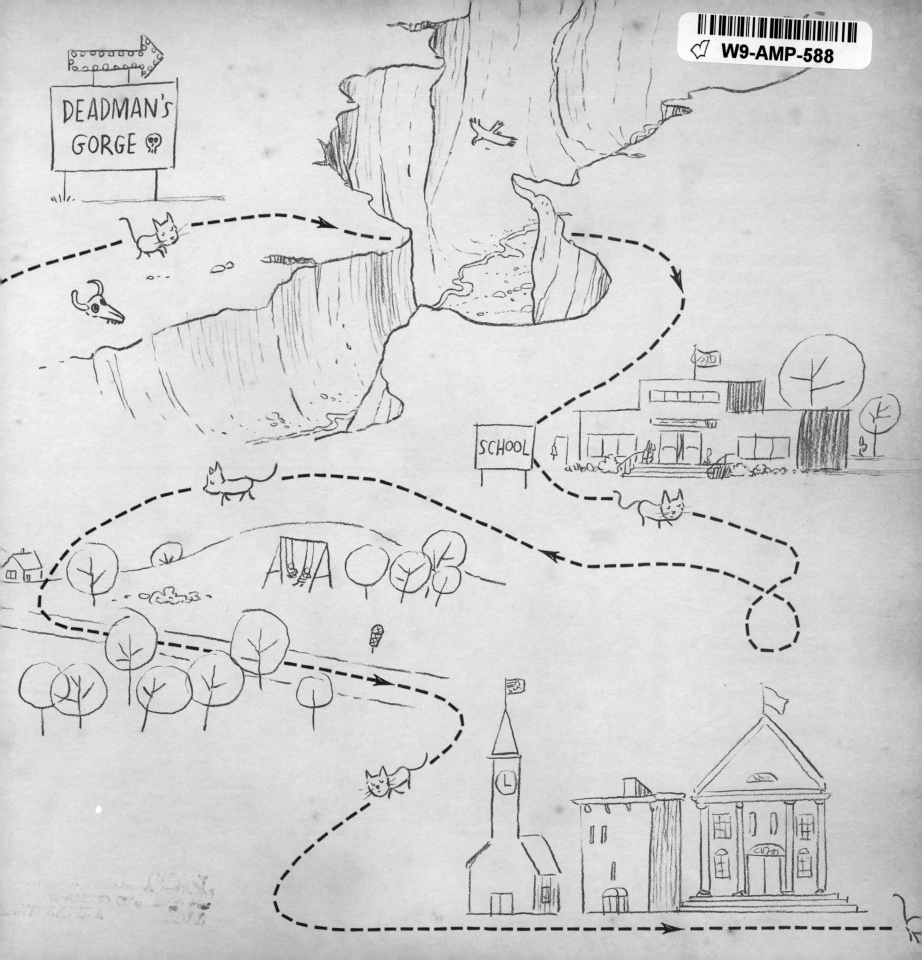

DEADMAN'S GORGE 💀

SCHOOL

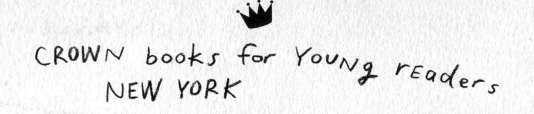

CROWN books for Young readers
NEW YORK

The CATaWampus Cat

Jason CArter EatoN

pictures by gus gordoN

For my mom,
the most catawampus cat I know.
Thank you for always showing me the
world from a unique angle.
—J.C.E.

For Pippin.
As faithful a cat as anyone
could ever hope for.
—G.G.

Text copyright © 2017 by Just Small Enough Films, Inc.
Jacket art and interior illustrations copyright © 2017 by Gus Gordon

All rights reserved. Published in the United States by Crown Books for Young Readers, an imprint of
Random House Children's Books, a division of Penguin Random House LLC, New York.

Crown and the colophon are registered trademarks of Penguin Random House LLC.

Visit us on the Web! randomhousekids.com

Educators and librarians, for a variety of teaching tools, visit us at RHTeachersLibrarians.com

Library of Congress Cataloging-in-Publication Data
Names: Eaton, Jason Carter, author. | Gordon, Gus, 1971–, illustrator.
Title: The catawampus cat / by Jason Carter Eaton ; illustrated by Gus Gordon.
Description: First edition. | New York : Crown Books for Young Readers, [2017] | Summary: The Catawampus Cat
    walked into town one day at a slant, and since then everyone in town is seeing their world with fresh eyes.
Identifiers: LCCN 2016008919 (print) | LCCN 2016035309 (ebook) | ISBN 978-0-553-50971-7 (trade) |
    ISBN 978-0-553-50972-4 (lib. bdg.) | ISBN 978-0-553-50973-1 (ebook)
Subjects: | CYAC: Cats—Fiction. | City and town life—Fiction. | Individuality—Fiction.
Classification: LCC PZ7.E137 Cat 2017 (print) | LCC PZ7.E137 (ebook) | DDC [E]—dc23

MANUFACTURED IN CHINA
10 9 8 7 6 5 4 3 2 1
First Edition

The CATaWampus Cat

arrived early

on a Tuesday morning . . .

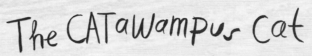

. . . slightly askew.

At first no one noticed. The town was a busy
town, and the people were busy people.

Tick, tick, tick, went the town.

Tock, tock, tock, went the people.

This is how it was every day, even Tuesday.

The first to see him was Mr. Grouse, the grocer, who tried to straighten him.

To no avail.

Fig. (i)   Fig. (ii)

"What's with that cat?" asked his wife, Lydia, who hadn't said a kind word to him in almost twenty years.
"You're asking me?" he said. "He must be hurt or curious or noticing something."

So they both tilted their heads.

And noticed something.

"That's where my wedding ring has been!" cried Lydia. "I haven't seen it in twenty years."

"Y'know," said Mr. Grouse sweetly, "from this angle you look exactly like you did the day we first met."

They kissed, and on walked the catawampus cat, still askew...

BARBER

ICE CREAMERY

tCHer

nest meats

37

. . . where he was spotted by the bored town barber, Bob Long, who was giving a woman a long bob. As he stared at the catawampus cat, he tilted his head and—

snip! —clipped at an angle.

"I love it!" shouted the woman.

And on walked the catawampus cat,
askew as ever . . .

. . . and passed a housepainter, who was busy painting the mayor's house. "What a dull, uncreative job," sighed the painter as he watched the cat walk by. It wasn't until he looked up at his work that he realized he'd been tilting his head.

TOM'S painting

"Brilliant!" exclaimed Mayor Meyer. "A work of art!"

When Captain Whizzbang, the town daredevil, saw the catawampus cat, he missed his jump over Deadman's Gorge.

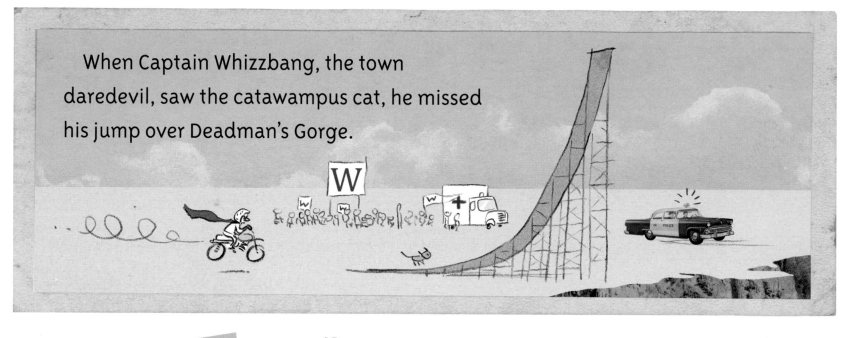

But landed instead in a geyser.
And set a new record for height.

When the town librarian, Miss Reade, saw the catawampus cat, she pulled the wrong book off the shelf.

SOUTH POLE

4

And then quit her job and set out
for adventure!

Even Bushy Brows Billiam, who always sat in the back of the classroom and never noticed anything, like what time it was or when class was over,

noticed the catawampus cat.

And discovered that he could see better than anyone if he just looked at the right angle. And Bushy Brows Billiam set off a chain reaction.

Soon people began to talk.

And then to tilt.

First their heads,

and then themselves,
just like the cat.

They rebuilt all the houses
so they were leaning,
and made all the
cars off-kilter.

Yponomeula

They spotted prized possessions they thought they'd never see again. And rediscovered old friends they thought they'd never know again.

Everyone was happy

and slanty

and catawampus.

Tock, tick, tickety, went the people.
Tick, tockety, tock, went the town.

Mayor Meyer decided to name the first Tuesday of the new year "Catawampus Cat Day" in honor of the remarkable cat. They all gathered in the lopsided town square and threw confetti at an angle from their uneven stage.

Oompah-oompoh, blared the off-key band as the catawampus cat walked onto the stage and stared out at the town, now completely catawampus.

"Well? What do you think of it?" asked Mayor Meyer excitedly.

"We're all different now, just like you."

Everyone held their breath as they awaited the cat's reaction.

Slowly, thoughtfully, the catawampus cat blinked twice . . .

. . . and stretched . . .

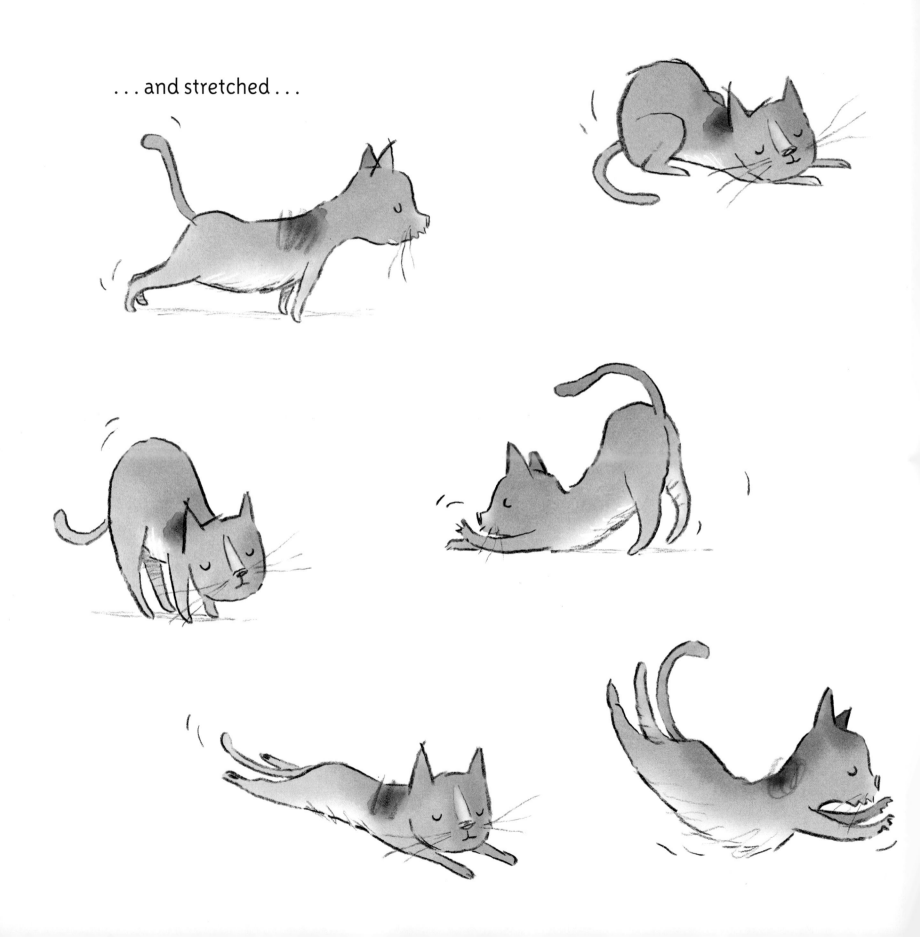

. . . and straightened himself out . . .

. . . and walked back out of town, once again uniquely catawampus.

10h. 24m. a.m.

shoes

BARBER